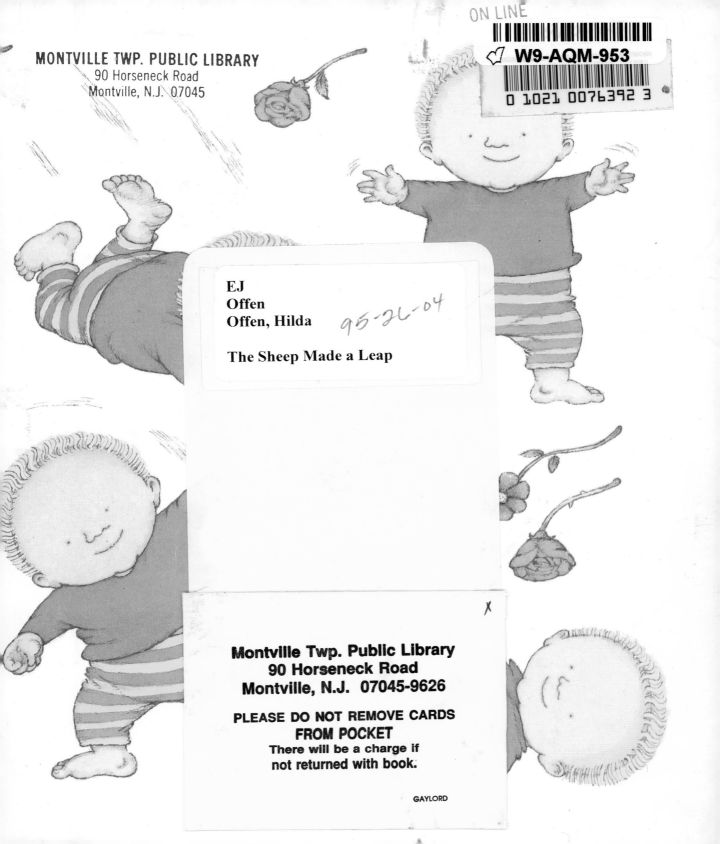

For Anna Lily Sidgwick

Copyright © 1993 by Hilda Offen
All rights reserved.

CIP Data is available.

First published in the United States
1994 by Dutton Children's Books,
a division of Penguin Books USA Inc.
375 Hudson Street, New York, New York 10014
Originally published in Great Britain 1993 by
Hutchinson Children's Books, an imprint of
Random House UK Limited
Printed in China
First American Edition
1 3 5 7 9 10 8 6 4 2
ISBN 0-525-45174-9

The Sheep Made a Leap

HILDA OFFEN

Dutton Children's Books · New York

Ladies and gentlemen—
the show's starting now!

Spread arms.

The audience clapped,

Grown-ups clap.

and my friends took a bow.

Bow.

First two little crows
pointed their toes.

Point toes.

Then two baby seals
rolled head over heels.

Do a somersault.

The sheep made a leap.

Jump in the air.

And the pig twirled around.

Twirl around.

The bear made us laugh

Everyone laugh.

when he fell to the ground.

Fall down.

The monkey stretched his arms out wide.

Stretch out arms.

The hippo swayed from side to side.

Sway from side to side.

When everyone stamped
and yelled for more,

Grown-ups stamp and yell.

the big gray elephant
rolled on the floor.

Roll around.

We all danced around
and kicked our legs high.

Dance around and kick legs.

Then the curtain came down,
and we all waved good-bye!

Wave.